THE Berenstain BEAR SCOUTS

and the

Humongous Pumpkin

THE Berenstain BEAR SCOUTS
and the
Humongous Pumpkin

by Stan and Jan Berenstain
Illustrated by Michael Berenstain

A
LITTLE APPLE
PAPERBACK

SCHOLASTIC INC.
New York Toronto London Auckland Sydney

ISBN 0-590-60386-8

Copyright © 1995 by Berenstain Enterprises, Inc. All rights reserved. Published by Scholastic Inc. APPLE PAPERBACKS and the APPLE PAPERBACKS logo are registered trademarks of Scholastic Inc.

12 11 10 9 8 7 6 5 4 3 2 1   5 6 7 8 9/9 0/0

Printed in the U.S.A.   40

First Scholastic printing, October 1995

• Table of Contents •

THE Berenstain BEAR SCOUTS
and the
Humongous Pumpkin

• Chapter 1 •

Now You See Him, Now You Don't

Bear Scouts Brother, Sister, Fred, and Lizzy were having a meeting in their secret clubhouse. No one else knew that the broken-down old chicken coop at the far end of Farmer Ben's farm was really the scouts' clubhouse. Nobody, that is, except Farmer Ben.

It had been a dirty, smelly place when Farmer Ben said they could use it for a clubhouse. But the scouts had worked hard cleaning it and fixing it up. Now it had a table and some chairs. The old

chicken roost was still there. But the
scouts had fixed it up with boards so they
could sit on it. They had made one wall
their "honor wall." The Official Bear Scout
Oath was the most important thing on the
honor wall. It said what the scouts had to
do to be good scouts. It was mostly about
being honest and fair, hardworking and
helpful. This is what it looked like and
this is what it said.

THE BEAR SCOUT OATH

A Bear Scout...
Is as honest as the day is long.
Admits when he or she is wrong.
Respects the creatures of creation.
Views TV in moderation.
Is never cruel, rude, or mean.
Plays the game fair and clean.
Does his or her best at school.
Following the golden rule,
always respects the rights of
    others,
    including even sisters' and brothers'.

Signed:
    Scout Brother
    ❀ Scout Sister ❀
    —Scout Fred—
    Scout Lizzy

Also hanging on the honor wall were the Bear Scout merit badges the troop had earned. They were pinned to a long ribbon that was tacked to the wall. The scouts had made the old chicken coop into a pretty nice clubhouse — at least from the inside. From the outside it still looked like an old chicken coop. But that was fine with the scouts. It helped keep their clubhouse a secret.

Today's meeting was about trying for another merit badge. "I say we should go for it," said Scout Fred. "You know what they say: 'Nothing ventured, vothing gained.' "

"When they say that," said Scout Sister, "what do they mean?" Sister and Lizzy were younger than Brother and Fred, and Sister thought that Fred sometimes used bigger words than he had to. Lizzy, who was sitting on the chicken roost, didn't seem to be listening. She was looking out the window at some birds in a tree. Suddenly the birds flew away. Somebody had frightened them. That somebody was Ralph Ripoff, Bear Country's leading crook and swindler. What was Ralph Ripoff doing out here in the middle of nowhere?

"Nothing ventured, nothing gained," said Fred, "means that if we don't *try* for the Creative Merit Badge, there's no way we're going to *get* it."

"All right," said Scout Brother. "That's enough arguing. Let's put it to a vote. All those in favor of entering the Spookiest Pumpkin Contest at the Big Pumpkin Festival, say 'aye.' "

Everyone except Lizzy said "aye." Lizzy was still looking out of the window. She had a puzzled look on her face.

"Lizzy," said Brother, "we're taking a vote!"

"About what?" asked Lizzy.

Brother explained about entering the

Spookiest Pumpkin Contest and trying to earn the Creative Merit Badge.

"Oh, sure," said Lizzy. "I vote yes — I mean 'aye.' But gang, something very strange just happened. I mean something *really weird*! You see that tree over there. Well, Ralph Ripoff was standing right beside it and ..."

"What's Ralph Ripoff doing out here in the middle of nowhere?" said Scout Sister.

"... and all of a sudden," continued Lizzy, "*he disappeared*!"

"Disappeared?" said Brother.

"That's right," said Lizzy. "He just plain old-fashioned disappeared!"

"But that's impossible!" said Scout Fred.

"Maybe it's impossible," said Lizzy, "but it happened."

• Chapter 2 •

Bear Country Above, Weaselworld Below

Many things that seem impossible really are. But others are not.

To see how Ralph was able to disappear right before Lizzy's eyes, let's turn the clock back a couple of minutes to just

before Lizzy saw him through the window.
Before Ralph came into Lizzy's view, he
was walking along, twirling his stick,
singing a song:

Ralph Ripoff
Is my name,
Ripping folks off
Is my game.
I lie, I cheat,
I borrow and beg,
I'm crookeder than
A dog's hind leg.
And what I like
Even better than honey
Is lots and lots
Of other bears' money!

As Ralph walked along, he looked this way and that. He looked at Farmer Ben's old chicken coop. But there didn't seem to be any chickens around. Ralph was on a mission so secret that he didn't even want to be seen by chickens. Even the birds in the tree ahead made him nervous. "Git! Shoo!" he shouted, waving his stick at them. The birds flew away.

Ralph was now standing belly-to-belly with the tree. After one last look around, he reached up and touched a small bump in the tree's bark. At Ralph's touch one side of the tree opened up like a phone booth. Ralph stepped in and the tree closed. Ralph had done exactly what Lizzy said. He had disappeared before her very eyes.

Once inside, Ralph braced himself. This was a trip he had taken many times. But no matter how many times he took it, he was never quite ready for that sudden

start and that awful feeling of falling.

It was even worse than The Space Drop at Grizzlyland, Bear Country's big theme park. Only instead of falling through space in a space car, he was falling through the earth in an earth car. Down through the high-speed tube plunged the earth car. Down, down it fell. It went faster and faster. It was all Ralph could do to keep from screaming. Finally it slowed and came to a stop with Ralph in a lying-down position. The moment it stopped, it popped open and dumped Ralph into a big basket marked "in." Ralph climbed out and dusted himself off. He faced a small, yellow-eyed creature, seated in a great carved chair behind a great carved desk.

"Chief," said Ralph. "We've got to stop meeting like this."

"Welcome to Weaselworld," said Weasel McGreed, head of all the weasels.

• Chapter 3 •

Whatever Happened to "All for One, and One for All"?

"Lizzy, are you sure you saw Ralph standing next to this tree?" said Scout Brother.

The scouts had left their chicken coop clubhouse and come to the place where Lizzy was sure she had seen Ralph disappear.

"Of course, I'm sure," said Lizzy. "He was standing right here, and all of a sudden he was gone."

"Looks like a regular tree to me," said Scout Fred.

"And it feels like a regular tree," said Scout Sister, feeling the bark.

"Hello, there!" called Lizzy. The birds that had flown away were coming back. Most of them lit in the tree's branches. But some of them fluttered down to visit Lizzy. One even lit on her finger. That was the way it was with Scout Lizzy. She had a way with animals—animals of all kinds—from butterflies to bees, from pigs to porcupines. Why, Lizzy could even pet a skunk without getting skunked.

The Bear Scouts were a team and usually got along together very well. But each member of the troop had special abilities. Lizzy had her way with animals. Scout Sister was bold and spunky. Scout Fred was as smart as a whip. He was the sort of cub who read the dictionary and the encyclopedia just for fun. Fred's smarts came in handy sometimes.

Scout Brother was the leader of the

troop. He was its oldest member, but that wasn't the whole reason he was the leader. Mostly it was because he was thoughtful and sensible. Scout Brother was the sort of cub who looked before he leaped and thought before he spoke. He did his share of leaping and speaking, but only after he had done his best to figure things out. That's what he was doing now. Trying to figure out what to make of Ralph's "disappearance."

For starters, he was sure of only two things. First, he was sure that if Lizzy said she saw Ralph disappear, that was what she had seen. Lizzy may have been a bit of a dreamer, but there was no question about her eyesight. She could tell one bird from another a thousand feet away. Lizzy had very good ears, too, though Brother wasn't sure she could hear a mosquito around the corner a block away, as she said she could.

The second thing that Brother was sure of was that a large bear wearing a plaid suit and a straw hat and carrying a walking stick couldn't just "disappear." There had to be an explanation. But what was it?

"Lizzy," said Sister. "There's no way you could have seen Ralph disappear."

"I know what I saw," said Lizzy.

"I say you were daydreaming," said Sister. "You just *thought* you saw Ralph disappear."

"I was not daydreaming!" said Lizzy.

"Yes, you were!" said Sister.

"I was not!" shouted Lizzy.

"Were! Were! Were!" shouted Sister.

"Not! Not! Not!" shouted Lizzy.

"Don't you shout at me, Lizzy Bruin!" shouted Sister.

"If you don't get out of my face, I'll do more than shout!" shouted Lizzy.

"Hey, wait a minute," said Scout Fred, stepping between them. "You two are supposed to be best friends."

"That's right," said Brother. "Bear Scouts are supposed to get along with their fellow bears. It says so right in the Bear Scout Oath. And whatever happened to 'All for one, and one for all'?"

That was the Bear Scouts' slogan. They got it from a book that Fred had read. The book was called *The Bear Musketeers*. It was about some soldiers from olden times. They used to cross their swords and shout,

"All for one, and one for all!"

Of course, the Bear Scouts didn't have swords. They looked around for something to cross. All they could find were broken-off branches. The scouts crossed their branches. "All for one, and one for all!" they shouted. The bears' slogan echoed across the rolling hills of Farmer Ben's farm.

• Chapter 4 •

Lots to Do

The scouts looked at the tree carefully. They looked all around the tree. But they couldn't find anything the least bit strange.

"Brother," said Scout Fred. "You haven't said what you think about Ralph's disappearance."

"Well," said Brother, "I've been thinking about it. And to tell you the truth, I don't know what to think. ..." Then, as so often happens when you're trying to figure out something really hard, just when you are about to give up an answer comes to you in a flash.

"The weasels!" said Scout Brother.

"The weasels?" said Scout Fred. "You mean that gang of weasels who are supposed to live underground and are always plotting to steal Bear Country from the bears?"

"That's just stuff that grown-ups tell cubs to scare 'em into being good," said Scout Sister.

"S-s-sure," said Scout Lizzy with a shiver. "Like the bogeybear, and the goblins that'll get you if you don't watch out."

"It was just a thought," said Brother.

But it was more than a thought. Brother had been hearing about the underground weasel gang for a long time. Especially from Grizzly Gramps.

Gramps had a whole scrapbook of bad things that happened. Things that Gramps thought were caused by the weasels. Like when all the honeybees got sick and stopped making honey. Or when the salmon in Great Grizzly River went belly up and died. But nobody took Gramps's ideas seriously. Not even Gran.

"Come on, gang," said Brother. He headed down the road. "We've got lots to do."

"Like what?" said Scout Sister as she and the rest of the troop hurried to catch up.

"First," said Brother, "we've got to stop off at Scout Leader Jane's and get her

okay on trying for the Creative Merit Badge. Then we've got to see about getting some pumpkins to carve for the Spookiest Pumpkin Contest. It's not going to be easy to win that contest. There were some pretty spooky pumpkins last year."

"Y-y-you're telling me," said Scout Sister, with a shiver. Though Sister was bold and spunky about most things, she was a little nervous about spooky things. Sometimes her fellow scouts teased her about it.

"I think we should carve a really scary witch," said Scout Lizzy. She made a scary witch face at Sister and bent her fingers to look like claws.

"I think we should carve a Frankenbear Monster," said Scout Fred. He leaned his head to the side and dragged his foot like the Frankenbear Monster.

"That'll be enough of that!" said Scout Sister.

Now it was Brother's turn. "I think we should carve a vampire," he said, showing his teeth. "Ah, vat a lovely neck you have, my dahling," he said in a vampire accent.

"If you don't cut it out," said Sister, bunching up her fists, "I'll flatten the lot of you!"

The other cubs threw up their hands and backed away in mock fear. But then Sister broke into a giggle. Soon they were all laughing as they walked along.

"After we get our merit badge okay from Scout Leader Jane," said Brother, "I want to stop off at Grizzly Gramps's."

"What for?" asked Scout Lizzy.

"What for?" said Brother. "Guess I can stop off at my own grandfather's if I want to."

• Chapter 5 •

Sealing the Deal

As the Bear Scouts walked along the
sunny Bear Country road, far below a
very strange pair was walking along one
of the spooky tunnels of Weaselworld.
They cast spooky shadows every which
way as they moved along the torchlit
tunnel. There were big broad shadows for
Ralph Ripoff and short skinny shadows
for Weasel McGreed. Armed weasel guards
stood at the ready along the tunnel walls.

"Are you sure you weren't seen?" said
Weasel McGreed.

"I'm sure, chief, I'm sure," said Ralph.

Though it was cool deep underground, Ralph was in a sweat. "There's no way I was seen, chief. This spot is way out in the middle of nowhere. It's way out on the edge of Farmer Ben's farm. The only building around is a broken-down old chicken coop. I mean, there aren't even any chickens around. There's no way I could have been seen. I'd stake my life on it."

"And so you have," said McGreed, his

fierce little yellow eyes gleaming in the torchlight. "This Farmer Ben of whom you speak—does he not grow pumpkins?"

"Oh, sure, chief," said Ralph. By now the sweatband of Ralph's straw hat was soaking wet. He took off his hat and fanned himself with it. "Farmer Ben is a fine pumpkin grower. The best in all Bear Country. Grows beautiful pumpkins. He's won first prize in the Big Pumpkin

Festival six years in a row. Not only are Ben's pumpkins big, round, and orange, they're ... "

"Stop jabbering," snapped McGreed, "and tell me why you have not chosen this Farmer Ben for our little experiment."

"Sure, chief, sure," said Ralph. "Two reasons. First, you said it had to be high ground. It's Papa's pumpkin patch that has the high ground. Overlooks the whole valley. Second, Farmer Ben is a mean, suspicious old cuss. He's the sort who counts his fingers after you shake hands with him. Papa, on the other hand, is a pushover, a natural born sucker. You could steal his underwear before he even felt a draft."

They had come to the place where Ralph had arrived earlier. Next to the big "in" basket, there was a basket marked "out."

"But, chief," said Ralph, "what's this

little experiment all about? Why do you need high ground? And what does it have to do with pumpkins? I mean, I like pumpkins as well as the next fellow. There's pumpkin pie, especially with whipped cream, and pumpkin bread and pumpkin pudding . . ."

Weasel McGreed had had enough. "Away with this jabbering fool!" barked McGreed in a low but fierce voice. "Get him out of here!"

The armed weasel guards crowded around Ralph. They started pushing him toward the "out" basket.

"But, chief, haven't you forgotten something?" said Ralph, holding his hand out.

"Pay the jabbering fool," said McGreed.

A henchweasel gave Ralph a bag of money.

"Easy, guys! Easy!" said Ralph. "I'm leaving! I'm leaving! I don't mean to be pushy, chief, but don't you think we ought to seal the deal with a handshake?"

McGreed held his hand out for a brief shake. Ralph climbed into the "out" basket. The moment he settled himself into the earth car, it closed and Ralph was gone.

"I want that fool watched every minute," said McGreed.

"Yes, master," said the head hench-weasel.

Then Weasel McGreed sat in the great carved chair behind the great carved desk. As he did so, the head of all the weasels, ruler of Weaselworld, held up his hand and started counting his fingers.

• Chapter 6 •

Mighty Clever These Weasels

Suppose the Bear Scouts had waited at the trick tree a bit longer. Would the mystery have been solved? The answer is no. That was because one of the trickiest things about the trick tree was its periscope. It was a thing you could look through and make sure nobody was around before you stepped out of the tree.

Mighty clever these weasels, thought Ralph as he checked to see if the coast was clear. Sure that it was safe, Ralph pressed a spot on the wall of the earth car. The tree opened and Ralph stepped out into the bright sunlight.

Too darned clever, thought Ralph as he walked along. Scary little guys. Especially that McGreed. Those nasty little yellow eyes seemed to look right through you. Maybe working for them wasn't such a great idea. If anybody found out about it I'd be in big trouble, thought Ralph. But their money was good. Real good. He squeezed the bag of money in his pocket and felt much better. He did a little jig of joy. Ralph was never so happy as when he was about to trick somebody. Playing old Papa Q. Bear for a sucker would be pure pleasure. But what about the weasels? What were they up to?

Ralph reached into his other pocket. He took out a small envelope. He shook it over his open hand. A single seed fell out. It looked like an ordinary seed. But wait a minute. When Ralph turned his hand a bit, the seed seemed to glow. The glow

worried Ralph. He put the seed back in
the envelope and returned it to his pocket.
What *were* these weasels up to?

The Bear Scouts settled their business
with Scout Leader Jane very quickly. Jane
was always glad to see her troop. But it
was fall break and Jane was busy mark-
ing school papers. Some of those papers

may have been Sister's and Lizzy's. Jane was a teacher at Bear Country School, and Sister and Lizzy were in her class.

"Your Creative Merit Badge plan sounds fine to me," said Jane. She opened the troop record book. "But my records say you still owe me a sleep-out." The troop had been working to earn the Sleep-out Merit Badge. To earn it they would have to have three sleep-outs in one month. So far they had two.

"We're going to be pretty busy, Scout Leader Jane," said Brother, "but we'll do our best to work it in."

With that, the scouts said good-bye to Scout Leader Jane and headed for Gramps and Gran's house.

• Chapter 7 •

More Like a Nightmare

The scouts followed their noses to Gramps and Gran's house. "What's that wonderful smell, Gramps?" called Scout Sister.

Gramps and Gran's house was a great place. It had all sorts of nooks and crannies, porches and towers. The scouts didn't know which was more interesting, the basement or the attic. They were both filled with wonderful old things. The most interesting room in the house was Gramps's den. That's where Gramps worked on his many hobbies. He collected stamps. He made ships-in-a-bottle. He carved amazing little monkey statues out of peach pits.

But let's not forget Gran's kitchen where that delicious smell was coming from.

"As you might expect," said Gramps, "that's the smell of the pumpkin pies Gran's making for the pumpkin festival. This year she's entering four kinds: plain, spicy, with nuts, and with raisins."

"Gran's a sure winner," said Scout Fred, breathing in the great smell.

"Maybe," said Gramps. "But the pie contest is gonna be tough this year. I hear
there are some great smells coming out of
Widder McGrizz's kitchen, too. And don't
forget Mrs. Ben. She's got her pick of
Farmer Ben's best pumpkins. By the way,
Brother, has your papa given up on the
idea of beating Farmer Ben for the biggest
pumpkin prize?"

"No, sir," said Brother. "He sure hasn't.
He says it's going to be his year to win the
big prize."

"That's not gonna be easy," said Gramps. "After all, Farmer Ben is a professional."

"Papa knows that," said Brother. "So he's working extra hard. He's been studying up on pumpkin growing, reading books about it."

"That's right," said Sister. "He's even got this book that says you can make plants grow by talking to them."

"Talking to them?" said Gramps.

"That's right," said Brother. "And it seems to be working. At least he's got some fine-looking pumpkins growing in his patch."

"Well, I guess it can't hurt," said Gramps. "Speakin' of talkin'. Is this a social visit? Or have you cubs got something on your minds?"

"We do have something on our minds, Gramps. It's Ralph Ripoff."

"What's that crook up to now?" said Gramps.

"Disappearing," said Scout Lizzy. "Disappearing is what he's up to."

"Interesting," said Gramps, sitting in his rocker. "Tell me about it."

So Brother, Sister, Fred, and Lizzy all pitched in and told Gramps the story of Ralph's strange disappearance. Gramps rocked slowly as he listened. It wasn't until Brother used the "w" word that Gramps stopped rocking.

"Hmm, disappeared, you say. Right out in the middle of nowhere," said Gramps. "Yes, that *could* have something to do with the weasels."

"I *thought* so," said Scout Brother.

"You mean the weasels are real?" said Scout Fred.

"And not just something grown-ups have dreamed up to scare cubs with?" said Scout Sister.

"More like a nightmare," said Gramps.

• Chapter 8 •

Think Big! Think Round!
Think Orange!

It was true. Papa did have some pretty
fine pumpkins in his patch. And he *was*
talking to them. Papa's pumpkin patch
was on top of a hill. Just beyond Papa's
pumpkin patch was a cliff that looked out
over all of Bear Country. To the right was
the handsome tree house where Scouts
Brother and Sister lived with their mama
and papa. The Bear family's tree house

PAPA'S PERFECT
PUMPKIN PATCH

HAVE A
GOURD DAY!

was almost a home away from home for Scouts Fred and Lizzy. They slept over often.

There was a split-rail fence around Papa's pumpkin patch, and lots of signs. There was a big one that said "Papa's Perfect Pumpkin Patch" and smaller ones that said things like "Have a Gourd Day!" and "Farmer Ben, Say Your Prayers!"

To the left was Farmer Ben's great pumpkin field. Ben had thousands of pumpkins. They looked like great orange jewels resting on their bright green vines.

There was a sign on Ben's field, too. It said "Farmer Ben, King of Pumpkins."

We'll just see about that, thought Papa as he urged his pumpkins on. "Grow, my proud beauties! Grow! Suck in that beautiful sunshine! Reach your roots down into that yummy soil and drink up that delicious water, and grow! Think big! Think round! Think orange!"

Papa's pumpkin patch was small. Compared to Farmer Ben's vast pumpkin field, it was tiny. But Papa's patch had some pretty fine pumpkins growing in it — and some big ones, too.

Mama was watching from a tree house window. She was preparing her special pumpkin bread for the festival. Mama didn't think it was Papa's talk that was making his pumpkins grow. She thought it was his hard, careful work. Mama sighed. She did hope Papa would have better luck at this year's pumpkin festival.

• Chapter 9 •

Ralph's Favorite Sucker

"Well, so long, Gramps and Gran!" said Scout Brother.

"And thanks for that yummy pumpkin pie," called Scout Sister.

Gramps and Gran waved from their front porch.

"And thanks for filling us in on those weasels," said Scout Fred. "I think."

"I know what you mean," said Scout Brother.

"Yeah," said Scout Lizzy. "It's pretty scary."

"Well, if any of those weasels ever

bother me," said Scout Sister, "I'll pop him one right on the nose."

"Sure you will," said Brother.

As the troop headed home, the scouts looked nervously at the woods on both sides of the road. If what Gramps had told them was true, the weasels might be watching them at that very moment.

Coming toward the Bear family's tree house from the other direction was none other than the no-longer-disappeared Ralph Ripoff. There was a spring in his step and a twinkle in his eye as he rounded a bend and caught sight of the Bears' tree house. Just beyond it, Ralph could see Papa tending his pumpkin patch. The sight of Papa cheered Ralph so, that he broke into song.

"Ralph Ripoff
Is still my name,
And swindling suckers
Is still my game,
I've got more tricks
Than a dog has fleas,
And now, dear friends,
If you'll excuse me, please,
I see my favorite sucker
Right over there,
Otherwise known
As Papa Q. Bear!"

"Well," said Ralph in a loud jolly voice. "As I live and breathe. It's my great and good friend, Papa Q. Bear!"

"Hi, Ralph," said Papa. "I'm working on my pumpkin patch."

"And what a fine pumpkin patch it is!" said Ralph. "Your pumpkins are a lovely sight to see. And there's no doubt about it, my dear friend, you are sure to win second prize in this year's Biggest Pumpkin Contest at the Bear Country Pumpkin Festival!"

"No, Ralph. You've got it wrong," said Papa. "I'm gonna win *first* prize. I've had enough of second prize. And I've had enough of that show-off Farmer Ben. Calls himself the Pumpkin King. Humph! Well, I'm gonna show him. I'm gonna win *first* prize! Yes sir! *First* prize!

"Now, if you'll excuse me, Ralph. I've got to talk to — er, work on my pumpkins."

Papa began to smooth out the patch with a hoe.

"That's the spirit, Papa Q.!" said Ralph. "Go for it! Look fate in the eye! Dream the impossible dream!"

Papa stopped hoeing. "Impossible?" he said. "You think it's impossible for me to win first prize?"

"Well, of course, nothing's really *impossible*," said Ralph. "I suppose you *could* win first prize. Farmer Ben's pumpkins could be attacked by screw worm and dissolve into orange goo. Or the earth could open up and swallow his whole crop."

"You know those things aren't going to happen, Ralph," said Papa Bear. He sat down on a rock. "Tell me, Ralph. Have you seen the pumpkins Ben's planning to enter?"

"Indeed, I have," said Ralph. "Amazing things. Big as wagon wheels! The color of the setting sun.

"Well, I must be on my way," said Ralph.

Papa sighed a long sigh.

"I guess I'll just have to face it," he said, looking very sad. "There's just no way I'm gonna win first prize."

Ralph had started walking away. But he stopped in his tracks, as if he'd suddenly remembered something very important.

"*Wait a minute!*" said Ralph. He reached into his pocket and took out a small envelope. "*How could I have forgotten?*"

"Forgotten what?" said Papa.

"This!" said Ralph. He looked this way and that, as if he were about to tell a big secret. He shook the envelope over his hand. A single seed fell out.

"A pumpkin seed," said Papa.

"But *what* a pumpkin seed!" said Ralph. "You see, I happen to have a cousin in Big Bear City who is a pumpkinologist."

"A pumpkinologist?" said Papa.

"That's a pumpkin expert," said Ralph. "This, my friend, is a whole new breed of seed."

"It glows," said Papa.

"It glows," said Ralph, "because this little old pumpkin seed is going to grow into . . ."

". . . a sure-fire guaranteed first-prize winner!" said Papa. "Lemme buy it, Ralph! Lemme! Lemme! Lemme! *Please!*"

Ralph put the glowing seed back into its envelope.

"I'm afraid it's not for sale," said Ralph.

"Not for sale?" said Papa.

"No," said Ralph. "But, my friend, it's yours as a gift." He handed Papa the small envelope.

Papa was speechless. He stared at it as if he had never seen an envelope before.

"G-g-gee, Ralph," said Papa. "I don't know what to say, except thank you, thank you, thank you! I'm gonna plant 'er right now!"

Papa fell to his knees and began digging a small hole.

"Hold on, Papa! Hold on!" said Ralph. "The planting instructions are printed on the envelope."

Papa got up. He began reading the instructions. "'For best results, this seed must be planted at sundown, no later, no earlier. It must be planted three inches deep, no less, no more . . .' Hey," said Papa. "This must be some seed."

"And," said Ralph, "it's going to grow into some pumpkin."

"A pumpkinologist, you say," said Papa.

"That's right. Graduated from Pumpkin University. Well, I must be on my way."

Ralph had looked down the road and seen something that made him nervous. Those pesky Bear Scouts were coming.

"Oh, yes, Papa," added Ralph. "That

first-prize pumpkin seed must be our
secret. If it gets out that I gave it to you,
my cousin could lose his job."

"Mum's the word," said Papa. He put
a finger on his closed lips.

"Well, ta-ta," said Ralph. Then he
hurried away.

• Chapter 10 •

Follow That Crook

"Hey," said Scout Sister. "Isn't that Ralph talking to Papa right now?"

Even though the scouts were a distance away, they could tell it was Ralph.

"That's Ralph, all right," said Brother. "Come on! We'd better get over there before he sells Papa the sky."

Brother had good reason to worry. Ralph had pulled some pretty raw deals on Papa. There was that honeybee hypnotizer he had sold Papa. It turned out it was just an old eggbeater. Papa had gotten pretty badly stung on that deal. Then

there was that driveway topping that
never dried. It was like black chewing
gum and stuck to everybody's feet.

Ralph was long gone by the time the
out-of-breath Bear Scouts reached Papa's
pumpkin patch.

"W-what were you and Ralph talking
about, Papa?" puffed Scout Brother.

"Nothing special," said Papa. "We were
just passing the time of day. He admired
my pumpkins, of course, and wished me
luck in the Biggest Pumpkin Contest."

"Uh-huh," said Brother.

The scouts looked around. They didn't
see any honeybee hypnotizers or cans of
black chewing gum. But they were still
worried. They moved a distance away and
put their heads together.

"I don't like the looks of it," said Scout
Brother.

"I think Ralph is pulling some kind of
trick on Papa," said Scout Sister.

"I say let's follow him," said Scout Fred. "Maybe he'll give something away."

"Come on!" said Scout Lizzy. "We'll cut across the field. We'll catch up to him and watch him from behind the dry wall."

Within minutes the Bear Scouts were crouching behind the wall that lined the road.

"Here he comes," hissed Scout Sister.

Ralph was quite a sight with his straw hat, flashy suit, and walking stick. His stick flashed in the sunlight as he twirled it. Ralph looked like he didn't have a care in the world as he walked along. And then it happened! The road just seemed to open up and swallow Ralph the way a trout would a fly.

"*Did you see that?*" said Sister.

"I saw it," said Fred. "But I don't believe it!"

"See?" said Lizzy. "That's what happened before. I *told* you I wasn't seeing things!"

"Come on!" said Brother. "Let's check out that spot in the road!"

• Chapter 11 •

"Glumpf! Glumpf!" said Ralph

Far below, deep in the weird underground world of the weasels, Ralph was shooting feet first into the same "in" basket that he had visited earlier. Only this time he was badly shaken. His suit was mussed and he'd lost his hat and stick. As he tried to get up, the stick shot out and poked him, and his hat landed on his head crooked.

"What's going on, chief? Is this any way to treat a trusted employee?" said Ralph.

"Mind your manners, fool," said Weasel McGreed, who was standing by with a gang of armed henchweasels. "I have questions for you, and you had better have the right answers."

"But, chief, look at this suit. I just had it cleaned and pressed," said Ralph as he climbed out of the basket.

"Question one," said McGreed. "Have you carried out my orders to the letter?"

"Absolutely, on the nose, to the letter," said Ralph.

"This Papa Bear has accepted the seed as planned?"

"Yes," said Ralph. "But I gotta ask you, chief. What's this all about? I've got a right to ..."

"Hush, you fool!" snapped McGreed. "And you're sure he will follow your instructions to the letter?"

"I'm sure," said Ralph. "Old Papa's tongue was hanging so far out for that first prize. ..."

"*Tie him and gag him!*" cried McGreed.

Quicker than you can say "welcome to Weaselworld," the weasels had Ralph tied and gagged.

"Glumpf! Glumpf!" said Ralph.

"Trusted employee, indeed!" said McGreed to the struggling Ralph. "You are not worthy of trust. You are a blabber-mouth! A loose cannon! A mindless twit! I can't risk your dropping even the smallest hint of our little experiment. So you'll be our 'guest' until it's completed. *Take him away!*"

"Glumpf! Glumpf!" said Ralph as the weasel gang pushed him along the tunnel.

"Speaking of cannons," said McGreed, "are ours in readiness?"

"All is in readiness, master," said the chief henchweasel.

Meanwhile, back up in Bear Country, where the road had swallowed Ralph the way a trout swallows a fly, the Bear Scouts were studying the spot where he had disappeared.

"Look!" cried Scout Sister. "A trapdoor in the road!"

"It says BCEC on it," said Lizzy. "Doesn't that stand for 'Bear Country Electric Company'? I don't get it."

"Maybe you don't get it," said Scout Brother, "but Ralph did."

"You mean . . ." said Sister.

"That's *exactly* what I mean," said Brother, hardly moving his lips. He began walking away. "Come with me. That trapdoor has a lot more to do with the weasel company than with the electric company. And don't look around!"

"Why not?" said Fred.

"Because," said Brother, "we weren't the only ones watching Ralph. The weasels were watching him, too. That's the only way they could have worked that trapdoor at the exact moment he was walking on it."

"I know Ralph is a crook," said Fred. "But I'll never forget his awful scream when he disappeared."

Brother led the troop back over the dry wall and into the field.

"Now here's the deal," said Brother. "Just as sure as one plus one equals two, one disappearing Ralph plus another disappearing Ralph equals . . ."

"Weasels!" agreed the troop.

"Right," said Brother. "So we don't want to fool around with that trapdoor. It could be dangerous."

"This is getting scary," said Scout Lizzy.

"Maybe we should tell our parents, or Scout Leader Jane," said Fred.

"Or the police," said Sister.

"I don't think so," said Brother. "Not just yet. They'll just see where it says Bear Country Electric Company and laugh at us."

"But what are we going to do?" said Fred. "I know Ralph is a crook and all, but ..."

"We're *doing* it," said Brother. "I think that tree out in the middle of nowhere may be the answer. We'll see if we can figure out how it works. Then we'll go to the police."

The Bear Scouts broke into a run.

• Chapter 12 •

A Tummy-Turning Trip

"It still looks like a regular tree to me," said Fred.

"And it still feels like a regular tree," said Sister.

Lizzy picked up a rock and knocked it against the tree. "Hmm," she said. "It does sound kind of hollow."

The scouts studied every inch of that tree's trunk. But no matter how hard they looked, they couldn't find anything strange.

"Well," said Fred. "We've studied this tree from top to bottom and we haven't found *anything*."

"Just a darn minute," said Sister. "We *haven't* studied this tree from top to bottom. We've just studied the bottom. Gimme a boost."

Scout Brother clasped his hands together and boosted Sister into the tree's branches.

"Hey! Look at this!" said Sister. "The end of this broken-off branch has a glass in it. Like something to look through."

"A periscope!" said Fred.

"Wow!" said Brother. "It's just like Gramps said . . ."

That's when Sister stepped on the bump in the bark and the whole side of the tree opened. The frightened scouts tripped all over themselves and piled up in some weeds. Scout Sister fell out of the tree. But she didn't get hurt, because she fell on her fellow scouts.

"See?" said Lizzy. "I *told* you . . ."

"I know! I know!" said Brother.

The scouts looked inside the tree.

"It's almost like a phone booth with no phone," said Sister.

"Or an elevator with no buttons," said Fred.

Sister, who was always a little too brave for her own good, stepped into the tree.

"Please, Sister!" said Brother.

"Don't be so chicken," said Sister. "Gimme another boost. There's a thing up there to look through."

It took the three of them to boost Sister up. But she never got to look through anything. Because with all four scouts inside, there was enough weight to start the earth car on its tummy-turning downward trip. The tree closed and the scouts were on their way to Weaselworld.

Down, down, down they fell. It was quite an experience. The Bear Scouts screamed all the way down.

After what seemed a long time, but was only seconds, the earth car slowed to a stop. As soon as it stopped, it opened and dumped the scouts into the "in" basket.

• Chapter 13 •

The Rumble of Cannons

The Bear Scouts huddled low in the "in" basket. They were hugging each other and holding hands. They could hear their hearts beating. They hoped no one else would. But there was little danger of that. The tramp, tramp of marching feet and the commands of the weasel captains echoed against the tunnel walls. The Bear Scouts could tell from the sound that the weasel armies were on the march. Huddled in the basket, the scouts remembered what Gramps had said: it was long past time for the weasels to make their move. The tramp, tramp, tramp faded in the distance.

One by one, ever so slowly, the Bear Scouts peeked over the edge of the basket. They could see the last of the weasel army marching out of sight.

"We've got to get away from here!" said Fred in a low voice.

"No," said Brother. "Now that we're here, we have to find out what we can. One thing looks sure. The weasels are going to make a move to take over Bear Country. How did Gramps say it: lock, stock, and honey pot! And we're the only ones who can do anything about it."

"But what can we do?" said Lizzy.

"At least we can look around," said Brother. "Come on."

There were no weasels in sight. The Bear Scouts climbed out of the basket.

"Our best bet is to follow the weasel army," said Brother.

So, staying close to the rough walls, they sneaked along the torchlit tunnel.

"If we're seen, we'll be done for," said Fred.

"That's a chance we'll have to take," said Sister.

The scouts were able to keep hidden in the shadows most of the time. But they were in plain view under the torches. They scurried past those places like bugs caught in the light.

Suddenly a door opened up ahead! Some weasels came out. The Bear Scouts held their breath and hid in the shadows. The weasels were talking in low voices.

The scouts tried to hear what they were saying, but they couldn't. When the weasels moved along the tunnel, the scouts tiptoed to the door. They heard sounds.

"It sounds like lots of hammering and sawing. They must be making something really big," said Sister.

Ever so carefully, the scouts opened the door just a crack. They peeked in. The weasels were making something really big, all right. But there was no telling

what it was. Dozens and dozens of weasels were working on big wooden parts of something.

"What do you think, Fred?" said Scout Brother.

"It looks like parts of a ship, or something," said Scout Fred.

"But that would be like building a ship in your basement, and then you can't get it out," said Scout Sister.

"Somebody's coming!" hissed Scout Lizzy.

The scouts plastered themselves against the wall. The door opened and out came a group of weasel soldiers. One of them wore a cape and a sword and had medals on his chest. He was barking out orders. The others were saying, "Yes, master! Yes, master!" Soon they were out of sight around a bend.

"That must be the guy Gramps told us about. McGreed, king of all the weasels," said Brother.

"I say let's go back to that earth car," said Fred. "What comes down must go up. Let's go back to Bear Country and warn somebody!"

"Warn them about what?" said Brother. "Warn them that there's a weird bunch of weasels marching back and forth who are building something. But we don't know what. No, we need to find out more. We need to find out exactly how they're planning to take over Bear Country."

The scouts moved on. There was another, much larger door up ahead. It was the kind that opens up like a garage door. There was a smaller door beside it. The scouts opened it a crack and peeked in. There were no weasels inside. But there was a weird-looking machine. It was huge! It had great wheels with studded truck tires and a tank as big as a small house. But the strangest thing about it was the part that pointed up in the air. It

looked almost like a giant Dustbuster
reaching for the ceiling.

The scouts heard a loud rumbling noise
in the tunnel behind them. They slipped
into the room with the strange machine
and watched. This time there was no
question about what they were looking at.
They were looking at *cannons*. Lots and
lots of cannons being pulled along by

teams of weasels. Behind the cannons were wagons piled high with cannonballs.

"*Now* can we go back to Bear Country and tell them what we saw?" said Scout Fred.

"I still wish we knew *how* the weasels are going to attack Bear Country," said Brother. "But you're right. It's time to go back. . . . But wait! What's that over there?"

Sister reached down and picked it up. "It's Ralph's walking stick!" she said. "I'd know it anywhere. And look there! If that isn't Ralph's straw hat, I'll eat it!"

The hat was kind of battered. It was on the floor beside a closet door. A muffled "Glumpf! Glumpf!" came from inside the closet. Brother opened the door. There was Ralph all trussed up like a Christmas turkey.

"Glumpf! Glumpf!" said Ralph.

• Chapter 14 •

Lucky for Ralph, Bear Scouts Are Good at Knots

First, the scouts removed Ralph's gag. "You crazy cubs!" he cried. "What are you doing here? If the weasels find you, you're done for!"

The scouts went to work on the knots that held Ralph tight.

"Never mind about that, Ralph," said Scout Brother. "What's going on down here? And what do you have to do with it?"

"Who, me?" said Ralph. "I don't have *anything* to do with it. I was walking along as nice as you please and *whammo,*

I'm down here tied up tighter than a tick . . . ! Oh, look what they did to my hat! Oh, dear!"

"Never mind about your hat!" said Brother. "What was going on between you and Papa today?"

"Nothing! Nothing at all!" said Ralph. "I swear on my sainted mother's lace shawl! It was about a pumpkin seed, that's all. The weasels paid me a modest sum to get Papa to plant a pumpkin seed. What possible harm could there be in a little pumpkin seed?"

"I don't know about pumpkin seeds," said Brother. "But there could be lots of harm in cannons."

"Lots of 'em!" said Sister.

"And cannonballs!" said Lizzy.

"And some kind of war machine!" said Fred. "And maybe even a warship!"

"Cannons?" said Ralph. "And cannonballs? And war machines? Goodness gracious me! This *is* serious! I don't know anything about that. But I do know we've got to get out of here and back to Bear Country. Look, you all sneak back to the earth car. Just get into it and it'll take you back up. It's automatic."

"What about you?" said Lizzy.

"Don't worry about me," said Ralph. "I know twenty-seven ways of getting out of here. But there's one very important thing. You must never tell anyone about me and the weasels. If you tell, the bears will tar and feather me and ride me out of town on a rail—a splintery rail! Now, get back to that earth car!"

• Chapter 15 •

The Good News
and the Bad News

With all the weasels moving in the other direction, the scouts got back to the earth car with no trouble. Ralph was right. It worked automatically.

The scouts were back up in Bear Country, safe and sound. But what to do? The scouts talked about it as they hurried back to the tree house and Papa's pumpkin patch.

"What do you think we ought to do?" said Scout Fred.

"It's hard to say," said Brother. "What

we have is a good news, bad news situation. The good news is that we found out that the weasels are gonna make some big move; the bad news is that we can't tell anybody about it."

"Why not?" said Sister.

"Because," said Scout Brother, "nobody will believe us. They'll say we're just a bunch of silly cubs making up stories. And I wouldn't blame them."

"But Ralph will back us up," said Scout Fred.

"No, he won't," said Brother. "He'll lie through his teeth. And I wouldn't blame *him*, either. You heard what he said. If the bears found out he was working for the weasels, they'd ride him out of town on a splintery rail. And I wouldn't blame *them*. No, we've got to cool it. We've got to keep our eyes and ears open and be ready for anything.

"What puzzles me," Brother went on, "is

what do cannons and soldiers have to do with a pumpkin seed and Papa's pumpkin patch?"

"Maybe," said Scout Fred, "that pumpkin seed is really a tiny radio sending out signals."

"A radio in a pumpkin seed?" said Scout Sister.

"It's possible," said Fred. "Scientists can do all kinds of stuff like that. I've heard they can fit a minicam into a green pea. And there's a video game coming out that you can wear in a ring."

"What kind of signals?" said Brother. Scout Fred shrugged.

"Hey, maybe we should tell Gramps," said Scout Sister. "He'd believe us."

"Yeah," said Brother. "But nobody will believe Gramps. Like in that old story, 'The Bear Who Cried Weasel.'"

As the Bear Scouts rounded a bend in the road, the Bear family's tree house came into view. There was Mama putting in some fall plants. On the high ground, there was Papa tending his pumpkin patch as calm as you please.

"You know what?" said Scout Sister. "I'm hungry."

"Hungry as a bear?" said Lizzy.

"You got that right!" said Sister. Mama always had cold milk and sandwich makings, and maybe even some fresh-baked cookies. The scouts put on speed and headed for Mama's kitchen.

• Chapter 16 •

The Humongous Pumpkin

After a meal of sandwiches and milk and cookies, the Bear Scout troop worked out a plan. They would act like nothing special was about to happen. The fact was, they couldn't figure out how anything *was* about to happen. At least not any time soon.

It was one thing for the weasels to play soldier down there in Weaselworld. But up here in Bear Country they wouldn't have a chance, cannons or no cannons. They would be up against *bears*. Why, powerful Papa could flatten the lot of them all by himself.

But, as Gramps said, the weasels were smart. So it was a good idea to stay on the lookout for signs of trouble. A key part of the scouts' plan was to keep a watch on Papa's pumpkin patch. That's where they would do the sleep-out they owed Scout Leader Jane.

Meanwhile, they got some small pumpkins from Papa and began getting ready for the Spookiest Pumpkin Contest. They set up in Papa's workshop. Lizzy was a very good artist. She made a witch sketch, a Frankenbear sketch, and a vampire sketch.

"Ooh!" said Scout Sister when she saw the sketches. Her fellow scouts thought it was pretty funny how brave Sister was about real things and how scared she was of things that weren't real.

When Lizzy finished her sketches, the scouts went to work carving the spooky pumpkins — except for Sister. She took the job of cleaning out the pumpkins' insides. She borrowed Mama's big ice cream scoop and went to work. Pretty soon she had a bucket overflowing with pumpkins' insides. It was a wet, gloppy, seedy mess.

The pumpkins were about half carved and looking pretty spooky when it began to get dark. The scouts set up their sleep-out camp right next to Papa's pumpkin patch. The troop had a delicious sleep-out supper. There's nothing yummier than hot dogs roasted on green sticks over a campfire and topped off with hot cocoa. Then they slipped into their sleeping bags and tried to go to sleep. It wasn't easy with all that was on their minds. But they'd had a long, hard day — and after a while they fell asleep.

Pretty soon Sister began to have a dream. But let's not mince words. Sister began to have a galloping rip-roaring nightmare! It wasn't the spooky pumpkins she dreamed about, the witch, the monster, or the vampire. It was the pumpkins' insides she dreamed about — those wet, gloppy, seedy insides. In the dream they rose up out of the bucket and formed into a wet gloppy weasel. A *giant* wet gloppy weasel. As soon as it formed, it began to chase Sister. She ran as fast as her legs could carry her. But the weasel monster kept getting closer and closer. The monster was just about to get her when she tripped over some kind of giant root and woke up.

But it turned out not only that the giant root was real, it was a giant *pumpkin* root. It had grown under her sleeping bag and lifted her up in the air. And it was still growing! That wasn't all that was still growing. Sister couldn't believe her eyes when she saw it. It was a humongous pumpkin. It was already as big as a house and it was still growing.

I must still be dreaming, thought Sister, but *maybe not!*

There was only one way to find out. Sister pinched herself *hard.* *"Ouch!"* she hollered.

Sister's "ouch" woke the others. Sister pointed at the humongous pumpkin. "I thought I was dreaming," she cried.

"It's no dream," said Brother.

"It's a living weasel nightmare!"

"You're right!" said Scout Fred. "It all makes sense now. The seed, the soldiers. That machine is a sucking machine. For sure, it's already sucking that pumpkin's insides into that giant tank!"

Lizzy had climbed up onto a giant pumpkin vine and was putting her extra-special good hearing to work. She put her ear to the pumpkin. "It's the weasels, all right. I can hear that one with the cape, the sword, and the medals, giving orders."

"That's McGreed!" said Brother.

"Look!" cried Scout Fred. Rows of square openings were being cut from the inside. "They're *gunports!*"

And, sure enough, cannons were poking out of the openings as soon as they were cut.

"That wasn't a warship they were working on," cried Fred. "It was a *war pumpkin!*"

The Bear Scouts knew that if they didn't do something all would be lost. And they had to do it *now*! With the weasels in control of the high ground, all of Bear Country would be under the weasel guns.

"We've got to do something!" cried Brother.

"But what?" cried Sister.

"What *can* we do?" cried Lizzy.

"Excuse me, friends," said Scout Fred. "But there was an ancient wise bear who said . . ."

"Please, Fred," said Brother. "This isn't the time for ancient wise bears. The weasels are about to take over Bear Country!"

"Lock, stock, and honey pot!" wailed Sister.

"Oh, dear! Oh, dear! Oh, dear!" cried Lizzy.

"I repeat," said Fred. "There was an ancient wise bear who said . . ."

"Fred, you shut up about ancient wise bears," cried Brother.

Scout Fred decided it was time to "show" rather than "tell." He picked up a long fence rail. ". . . an ancient wise bear who said, 'Give me a lever and a place to stand and I can move the world!'" He put one end of the fence rail under the pumpkin. Then he rested the rail on a rock and began pulling down on the long end. The humongous pumpkin began to tip just a little.

"How about four levers!" cried Brother.

Within seconds there were four fence-rail levers in place and four Bear Scouts pulling down on them.

"Heave ho! Heave ho!" shouted the scouts. The pumpkin was now tipping quite a lot.

Meanwhile, up in the tree house, the shouts of the scouts woke Papa. He went to the window to see what the noise was about and saw the biggest pumpkin the world had ever seen. The sight thrilled Papa down to his very toes.

It was the last "heave ho!" that did it. The humongous pumpkin tore loose — vine, roots, weasels, and all. It rolled to the edge of the cliff and crashed down into the valley with the biggest SPLOOSH ever heard in Bear Country.

It was still too dark to see what sort of mess it made or what happened to the weasels and their cannons. But the scouts really didn't care what happened to the weasels. What they cared about and were

proud of was that they had saved Bear
Country!

The Bear Scouts looked at each other.
They knew that this was a special
moment. It was time to say their slogan.

The fence rails were big and heavy, and it wasn't easy to cross them. But they managed to do it.

"All for one, and one for all!" they shouted.

Papa had thrown on his clothes and gotten outside just in time to see the humongous pumpkin roll off the cliff and crash into the valley. Papa rushed over to the great torn place where the pumpkin had grown.

"My pumpkin!" he cried. "My surefire, couldn't-miss, guaranteed first-prize-winning pumpkin! What happened to it?"

"Well, Papa," said Sister, taking him by the hand. "It just sort of tipped over."

"There'll be other pumpkins, Papa," said Brother.

"But not like that one," said Papa. "That pumpkin was ... *humongous!*"

"Papa," said Brother. "You've sure got that right."

ALL FOR ONE,   AND ONE FOR ALL!

• Chapter 17 •

The Best Good Deed

Papa came in his usual second to Farmer Ben in the Biggest Pumpkin Contest. The Bear Scouts came in only third in the Spookiest Pumpkin Contest. But that was good enough to earn the Creative Merit Badge. They also earned the Sleep-out Merit Badge, of course.

But the Bear Scouts not only did not earn a merit badge for saving Bear Country from the weasels, they couldn't even tell anybody about it. They wanted to, but Gramps convinced them that nobody would believe them. He convinced them of that by taking them to all the places where the weasels might have left a trace. He opened the electric company trapdoor. All that was down there was wires. As for that tree in the middle of nowhere — it was gone! They even checked out the valley into which the humongous pumpkin had splooshed. They couldn't find a trace.

"I told you," said Gramps. "That's the way it is with the weasels. They never leave a trace."

"Gee," said Scout Sister. "We did this great thing and nobody knows about it."

"*You* know about it," said Gramps. "And here's a little rhyme I'd like you to think about:

"There are good deeds large
And good deeds small,
But the good deeds which
Are best of all
Are those unknown
Except to us,
That win us no
Applause or fuss,
The deeds we feel
Deep inside,
In which we take
The greatest pride."

The scouts looked out over beautiful, bountiful Bear Country.

"I'll buy that," said Scout Brother.

"Me, too," said Scout Sister.

"Me, too," said Scout Fred.

"And so will I," said Scout Lizzy.

Then they headed for Gramps and Gran's for some of Gran's first-prize-winning pumpkin pie. It was delicious!

• About the Authors •

Stan and Jan Berenstain have been writing and illustrating books about bears for more than thirty years. Their very first book about the Bear Scout characters was published in 1967. Through the years the Bear Scouts have done their best to defend the weak, catch the crooked, joust against the unjust, and rally against rottenness of all kinds. In fact, the scouts have done such a great job of living up to the Bear Scout Oath, the authors say, that "they deserve a series of their own."

Stan and Jan Berenstain live in Bucks County, Pennsylvania. They have two sons, Michael and Leo, and four grandchildren. Michael is an artist, and Leo is a writer. Michael did the pictures in this book.

THE Berenstain BEAR® SCOUTS

by Stan & Jan Berenstain

Join Scouts Brother, Sister, Fred, and Lizzy as they defend the weak, catch the crooked, joust against the unjust, and rally against rottenness of all kinds!

Collect all the books in this great new series!

Don't miss the Berenstain Bear Scouts' first two exciting adventures!

☐ BBF60380-9 **The Berenstain Bear Scouts and the Humongous Pumpkin** $2.99
☐ BBF60379-5 **The Berenstain Bear Scouts in Giant Bat Cave** $2.99

© 1995 Berenstain Enterprises, Inc.
Available wherever you buy books or use this order form.

Send orders to:
Scholastic Inc., P.O. Box 7502, 2931 East McCarty Street, Jefferson City, MO 65102-7502

Please send me the books I have checked above. I am enclosing $_____ (please add $2.00 to cover shipping and handling). Send check or money order - - no cash or C.O.D.s please.

Name _____ Birthdate ___ / ___ / ___
                                                          M   D   Y
Address_____

City_____ State _____ Zip _____

Don't miss

Meet Bigpaw

"Okay, now. Move closer together," said the professor. He didn't have to ask the Bear Scouts to say "cheese" because they were already grinning like smile buttons. "Closer, so I get you all in the picture," said the professor, backing up a bit.

Scientists are often said to be absent-minded. But the problem with scientists—and Actual Factual was Bear Country's greatest scientist—is not that they are absent-minded. The problem is that they focus so hard on the problem of the moment that they forget to be careful. The professor's problem of the moment was getting all the scouts into the picture. So he kept backing up until he backed right off the edge of Table Rock.

"Professor!" screamed the scouts. Their smiles turned to looks of horror as they rushed to look over the edge of Table Rock. But instead of seeing the awful thing they expected—the sight of Actual Factual bouncing down the mountainside like a rag doll—they saw something much more shocking. A great hairy arm had reached out and caught the professor in a huge paw. The scouts stared in disbelief as the arm, the paw, and the professor were pulled back into the cave.

As one, the Bear Scouts remembered Gran's prediction.

"Bigpaw!" they said.